Nobody Likes a GOBLIN

:01
First Second

Published by First Second
First Second is an imprint of Roaring Brook Press,
a division of Holtzbrinck Publishing Holdings Limited Partnership
175 Fifth Avenue, New York, New York 10010

Library of Congress Control Number: 2015944387

ISBN: 978-1-62672-081-7

Our books may be purchased in bulk for promotional, educational,
or business use. Please contact your local bookseller or the Macmillan
Corporate and Premium Sales Department at (800) 221-7945 ext.5442
or by e-mail at MacmillanSpecialMarkets@macmillan.com.

First edition 2016
Book design by Danielle Ceccolini
Printed in China by RR Donnelley Asia Printing Solutions Ltd., Dongguan City,
Guangdong Province

Art created with india ink, Sakura Micron pens, watercolors, and
assorted brushes on Arches 140lb hot press watercolor medium.

10 9 8 7 6 5 4 3 2 1

TO BLACK STAG AND
THE BEEFY BOYS

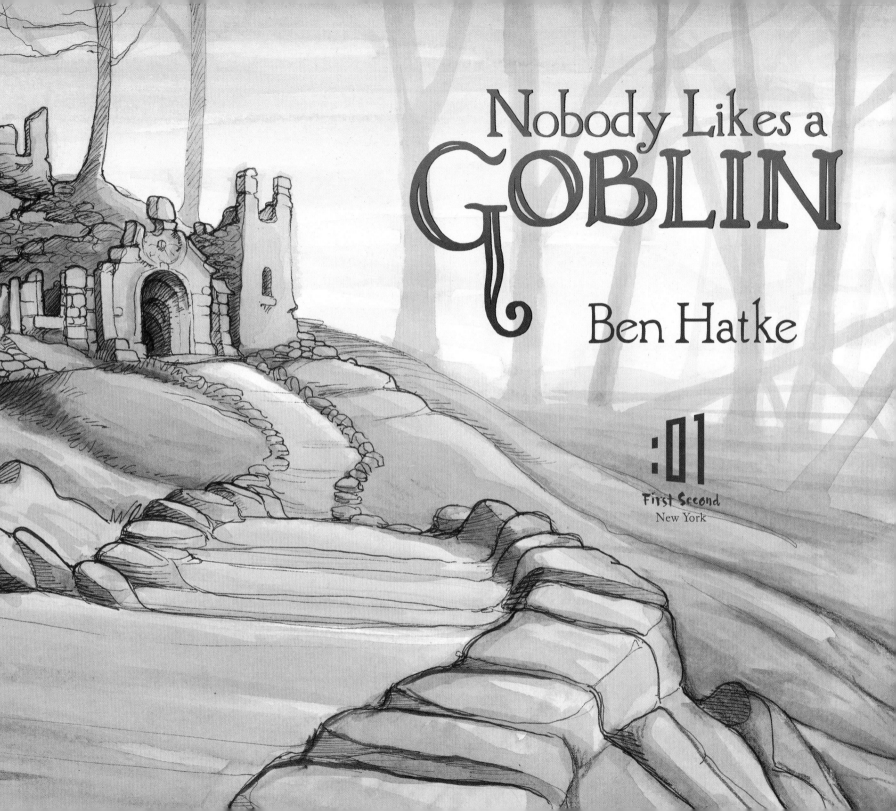

Nobody Likes a GOBLIN

Ben Hatke

:01

First Second

New York

Deep in a dungeon
the bats were sleeping soundly,

and Goblin woke to a new day.

He lit the torches.

He fed the rats.

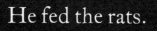

He gnawed on an old boot for breakfast,
and he thought about the day ahead.

"I think I'll go see Skeleton," said Goblin.

Skeleton lived in the Treasure Room and he was Goblin's Very Best Friend.

They counted bats, they played roll-the-dice, and Skeleton told Goblin stories from the days when he was a mighty warrior. He even let Goblin try on his old crown.

"Look at me!" said Goblin.
"I'm the Goblin King!"

But then came the sound
of boots on stone.

ADVENTURERS WERE STORMING THE DUNGEON!

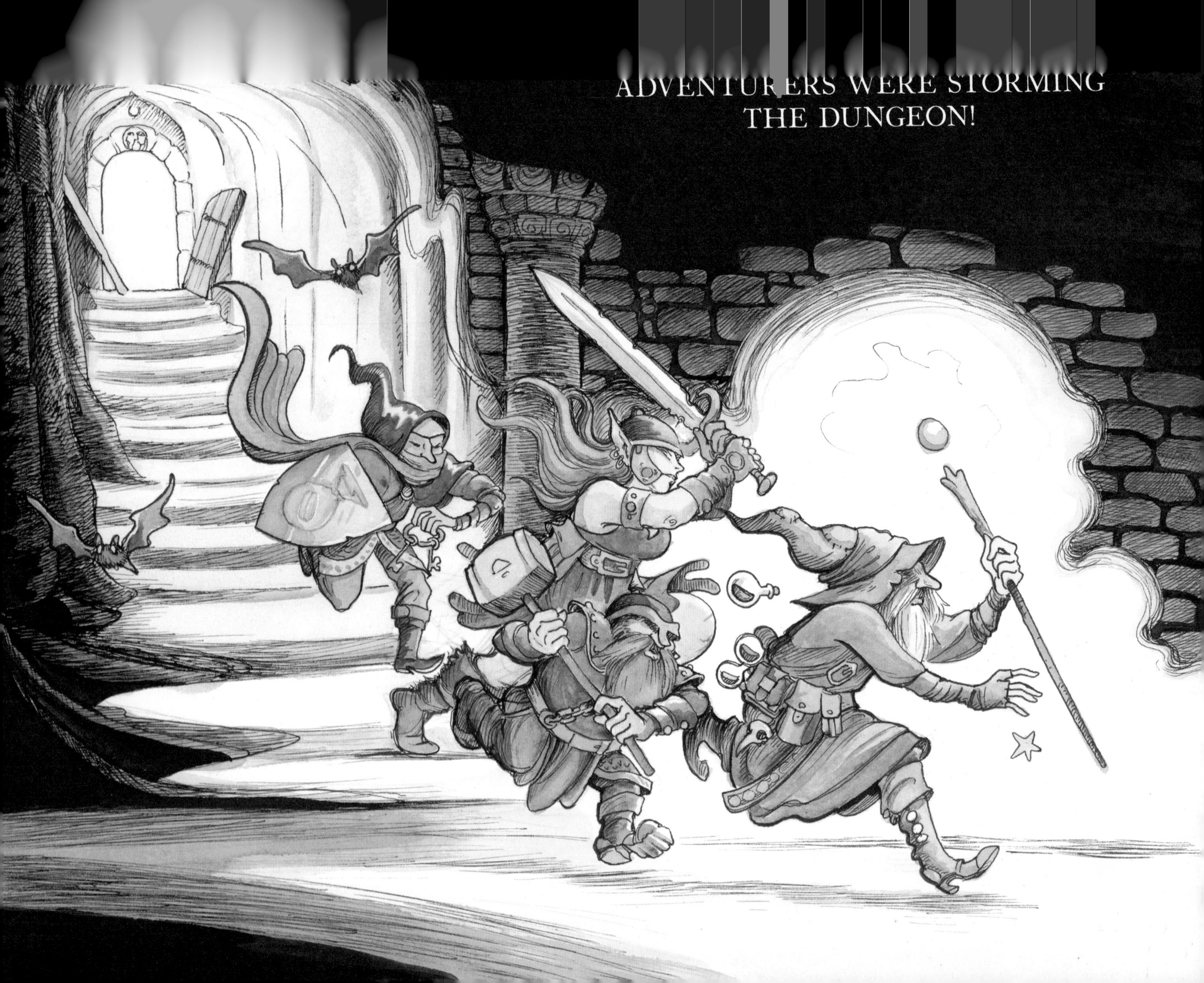

They scared the rats.

They knocked over the torches.

They plundered the pantry.

Goblin hid under his bed until
they went away.

The adventurers took everything.

They took the gold.
They took the maps, the books,
the gems, and the scrolls.

And they took Skeleton.

So Goblin put on his crown

and walked out into the wide
world to find his friend.

Goblin had one neighbor—a hill troll that lived in a cave nearby.
"I'm looking for my friend Skeleton," Goblin told him.

"I saw your friend," said the troll.
"He was with the adventurers who took my
Honk-Honk away over the mountains."

"I'll get your Honk-Honk
back," said Goblin.

"Be careful," said the troll.
"Nobody likes a goblin."

"I'll be okay,"
said Goblin.

And he walked up into the hills . . .

. . . and away over the mountains.

On the far side of the mountains Goblin met a farmer.
"I'm looking for my friend Skeleton," said Goblin.

"ACK!" shrieked the farmer.
"A FILTHY GOBLIN!"

And he chased Goblin down the road.

The farmer chased Goblin right through an inn full of elves.

"UGH!" said the innkeeper. "A disgusting little goblin!"

"Catch it!" cried the elves.

And they tried.

The farmer, the innkeeper, and the elves chased Goblin to the edge
of the Haunted Swamp, and there Goblin saw the adventurers pulling
a cartload of spoils. And sitting atop the treasure was—

"Skeleton!" shouted Goblin.

"GET THAT GOBLIN!"
shouted everyone.

Goblin grabbed hold of his friend and ran.

Goblin and Skeleton ran through the
Haunted Swamp until they passed a cave.

"We'll hide in here!"
said Goblin.

"They're looking for us," said Skeleton.
"They will find us soon."

"I know," said Goblin.

"Troll was right."

"Nobody likes a goblin."

"Well I like a goblin," said Skeleton.

And the two friends
sat together and waited
for their doom.

But then . . .

"Excuse me,"
said a voice from the back of the cave.

Goblin turned and saw many eyes staring at him from the darkness.

"Do you know who *else* likes a goblin?" said the voice.

"We saw your crown," said the other goblins.
"Are you the Goblin King?"

Goblin thought for a moment.
"Yes," he said.
"Yes, I am."

"We must defend the Goblin King!"
said the other goblins.

And they did.

The farmer, the innkeeper, and the elves ran for the hills.

And the adventurers, well,
they were never heard from again.

And so, Goblin and Skeleton and their new friends traveled
together back through the swamp,

up the road,

over the mountains,

down the hill,

and home
to the dungeon.

THE END.